D1608384

LAND OF LOTS

PLAN GILL

Written by Christian Carl
& Illustrated by Joyce Fan
With Chuck & Sue Willis

AuthorHouse™
1663 Liberty Drive
Bloomington, IN 47403
www.authorhouse.com
Phone: 833-262-8899

This book is printed on acid-free paper.

ISBN: 978-1-6655-2580-0 (sc)
ISBN: 978-1-6655-2579-4 (hc)
ISBN: 978-1-6655-2581-7 (e)

Printed in China.

Library of Congress Control Number: 2021909851

Published by AuthorHouse 07/21/2021

authorHOUSE

Lovelot was just a girl roaming through space.

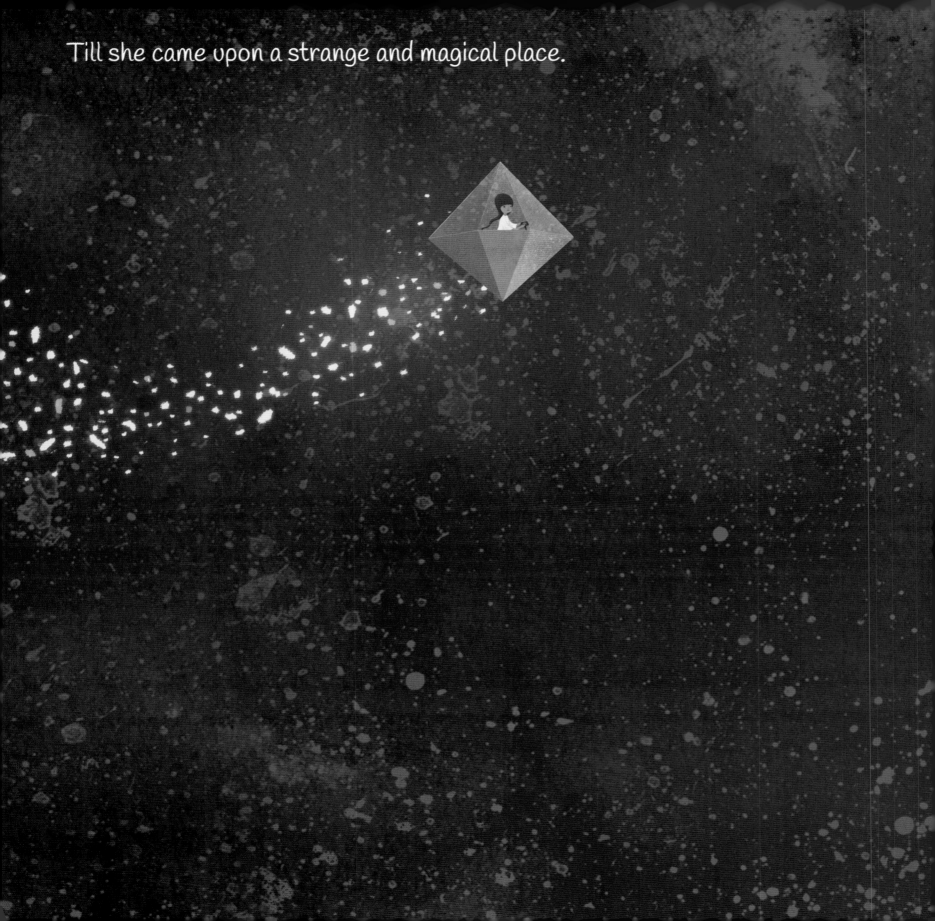

Till she came upon a strange and magical place.

She decided to take a closer look.

And so begins our second book.

She discovered the Oomlots who lived there.

One of those Oomlots was a fish named Gill.

He was known for running his mouth at will.

Today he had a tale to tell that was extra tall.

And he couldn't wait to tell not just one Oomlot, but all.

He thought Cubby should be the first to hear his tale.
But he was too busy hugging an Oomwhale.

He knew Dewey was always up for a good story.
But he was too busy rocking and roaring with Rory.

He thought if anyone would lend him an ear, it was Rudy.
But Peggy was keeping him busy on kitchen duty.

He thought Penny might like a good yarn session.
But she was too busy writing her name on all her possessions.

He wondered if Lovelot could tell him why no one seemed to care.
Because when an Oomlot needed her, she was always there.

While Gill walked away feeling good about Lovelot's plot.
She went off to have a word with every single Oomlot.

She asked Cubby to gather some very large boulders.
While she took a ride on his shoulders.

She asked Peggy to whip up a sweet surprise.
While Rudy thought of the mess and rolled his eyes.

She asked Rory and Dewey to stop their high kicks.
And give her a hand gathering some sticks.

She asked Penny to stop labeling for the rest of the day.
And help her knit some blankets straight away.

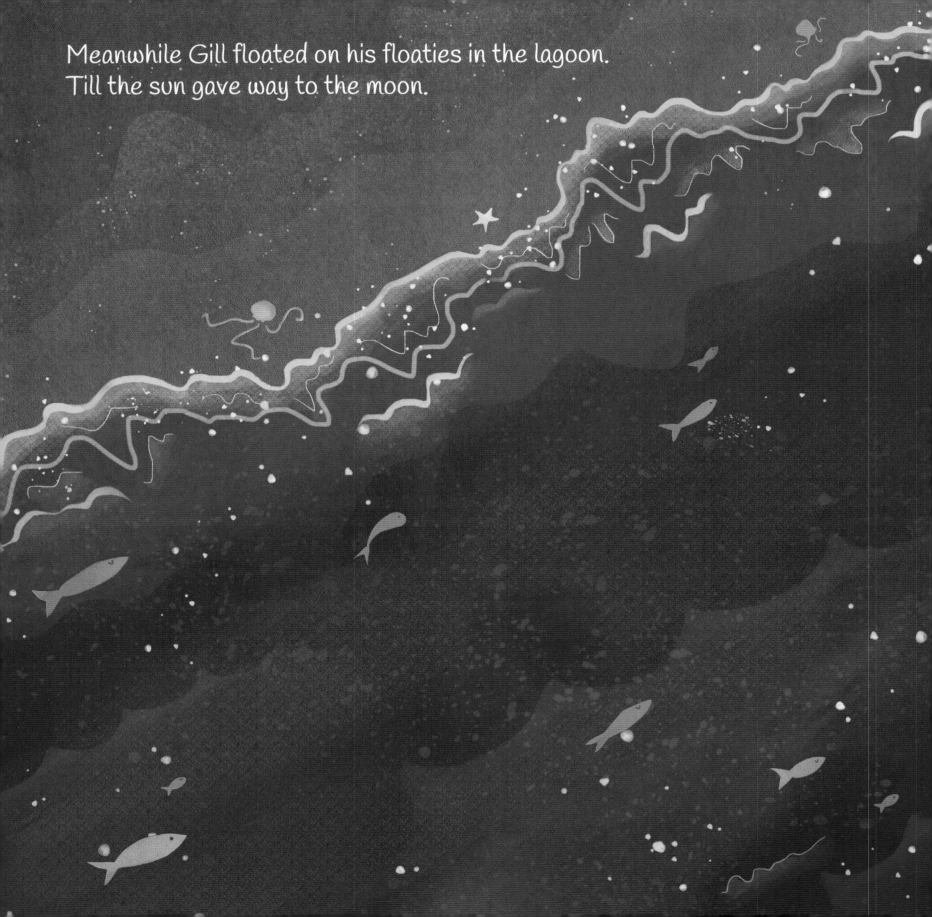

Meanwhile Gill floated on his floaties in the lagoon.
Till the sun gave way to the moon.

Everything was ready for Lovelot's plan.
While Gill made his way back to dry land.

The campfire was lit and everyone gathered 'round.
When Gill returned he couldn't believe what he had found.

They were all ready and waiting to hear his tall tale.
Cubby even invited the Oomwhale.

The stage was set and it was time for Gill to do his thing.
But he just sat there silently thinking...

He noticed the chirping of Oomcrickets filled the night.
And so talking right now just didn't feel right.

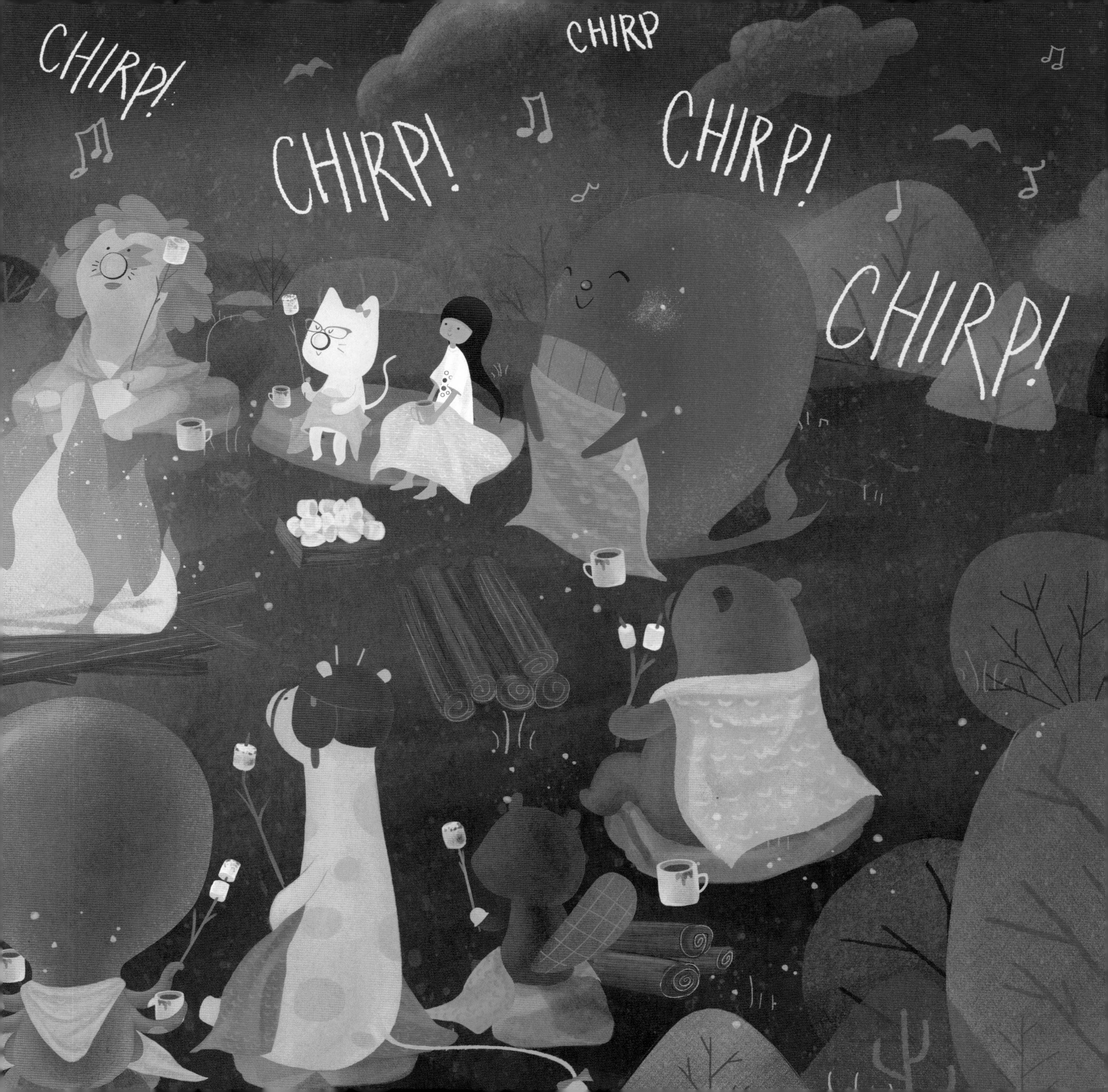
CHIRP!
CHIRP
CHIRP!
CHIRP!
CHIRP!

Lovelot gave Gill a knowing glance.
And each and every Oomlot began to dance.

Of course this was Lovelot's plan all along.
Who else do you think asked the Oomcrickets to break into song?

Psstt... P

Psstt...

Pss

Cubby loves to hug lots.

Penny loves to knit lots.

Paige loves to read lots.

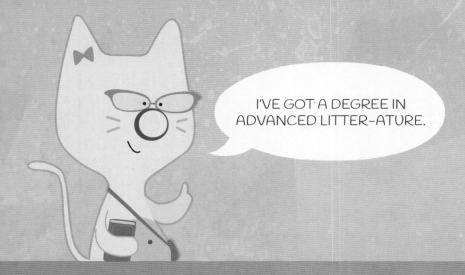

Rainy loves to garden lots.

Janie loves to explore lots.

Foggy loves to daydream lots.

Dewey loves to help lots.

Bucky loves to build lots.

Rudy loves to laugh lots.

Rory loves to roar lots.

Gill loves to talk lots.

Peggy loves to cook lots.

ABOUT THE CREATORS

Christian Carl

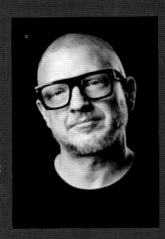

I've helped raise three kids ages 27, 17 and six. Though the world has changed a lot over nearly three decades of parenthood—one thing hasn't. Kids are impetuous, impatient, obsessive, selfish, clingy, loud, careless, moody, imaginative, loving, caring, beautiful, and oddly smart little beings who just need two things from us – patience and a plan. Land of Lots is a faraway planet, but it hits close to home for me. And I hope it does for you too.

Joyce Fan

A Hong Kong born, Portland Oregon raised artist. Her illustrative work is often reminiscent of her childhood imaginations and its whimsical adventures. Art, food, toys and music are among the many things that keep her creative juices flowing.

Chuck and Sue Willis

Together they have been in film and advertising collectively for over half a century and working with author Christian Carl on Land of Lots for what seems like a millennium. They hope the books bring you lots of laughs, learning and love.

We'd love to hear from you!
info@thelandoflots.com
www.thelandoflots.com